Mc KiDS
NEW KID
in SCHOOL

By Ellen Patrick

Illustrated by Alice Pederson

A GOLDEN BOOK • NEW YORK

Golden Books Publishing Company, Inc., New York, New York 10106

Dear Jessica,
We had a new kid in school today. His name is Jin. He is from China and doesn't speak English very well.

I like him but am afraid my friends will make fun of me if I am nice to him. What should I do?

Your pen pal,
Michael

P.S. Here is a picture of me and my dog Kareem.

→

Dear Michael,

The same thing happened to me when Angelita moved in down the street. Angelita is my best friend, but it didn't start out that way.

At first, everyone thought
Angelita was weird. She talks
with an accent because she's
from Mexico. She brings funny-
looking food for lunch, like these
rolled up things called tortillas. She
gets up early every day to go to
church. And she helps her grandma
take care of her four little brothers
and sisters after school while her
mom and dad are at work.

One day, Angelita asked me to sit with her at lunch. In her lunch box, she had a fried banana! She asked me if I wanted some. I wanted to try it, but I knew my friends were watching so I said, "Yuck, no. Only weirdos eat fried bananas." Then I walked away. But I felt bad for the rest of the day.

At recess, Angelita asked if she could play in the kickball game. "Okay, Banana Girl," they teased her. I sat by myself under a tree and watched. I was surprised that she played so well. She even kicked a home run!

On the way home, Angelita asked to sit next to me on the bus. T.J., a big bully in our class, sat behind us and made fun of her. I told him, "Leave us alone." That made T.J. mad. After I got off the bus, he yelled out the window, "Jess is a mess! Jess is a mess!"

I ran to my house, went upstairs to my room, and slammed the door. I cried and cried. When my mom asked what was wrong, I couldn't explain.

The next day at recess, some of the kids asked Angelita to be on their kickball team. She said she would play if I could be on her team, too.

"Okay, we'll take old Jess the Mess," said that big bully T.J.

I wanted to cry and run away, but Angelita hung onto my arm and said something in Spanish. Then she gave me a piece of gum.

Later, on the bus, Angelita asked me to come over after school. I even stayed for dinner! Angelita helped her grandma cook it. When her mom and dad got home from work, we had rice and beans, and those rolled up tortilla things.

Then Angelita's mom brought out a plate of — you guessed it — fried bananas! Angelita's mom told us that in Cuba, where she used to live, everybody loves fried bananas. In Spanish they call them "plantanos."

When Angelita's mom handed me the plate of bananas, Angelita told her, "Jessica doesn't like fried bananas." But I said, "I'll try one." Everybody was watching me. I didn't want to look dumb in front of Angelita's whole family.

Guess what? I liked the fried banana! A lot! Angelita thought that was so funny. She couldn't stop laughing. Finally, she said that if I liked them so much, she would show me how to make them — if I would show her how to make pizza.

Now Angelita and I do everything together. We ride the bus to school together, eat lunch together, and ride home together. She showed me how to plant tomatoes and sew a pot holder. I help her with her reading and writing in English.

Angelita did show me how to make fried bananas, but I didn't know how to make pizza. I asked my mom and she showed us how. (My mom makes the best pizza in the world, I guess because she's the best mom in the world!)

Angelita calls me her "amiga favorita." In Spanish that means I'm her best friend. I just call her Ange. That means she's my best friend, too.

For my birthday, mom let me have a sleepover with Angelita and two other friends, Chantal and Sabra. We played music and danced and stayed up really late!

For my birthday present, Angelita gave me a jacket she made all by herself (with a little help from her mom). On the back, her mom stitched the words: "Jess the Mess." It's my favorite thing that I own. I wear it to school every day.

When I asked Angelita one time why she was friends with me, she just laughed and said, "Because you are Jess, the Very Greatest Mess!" That made me feel good, the way she said it.

So, Michael, my answer to your letter is that you should make friends with the new boy, Jin. You never know — he might end up being your very greatest best friend,

Your pen pal,

Jessica

P.S. Here is a picture of me in my cool jacket with Angelita

P.P.S. Write again soon!

Meet The McKids®!

Kwesi Jin Sabra Michael Angelita Luis T.J. Chantal Katya Jessica

A Message for Parents

Children are never too young, or too old, for books. Educators agree that reading aloud to your children is the most important thing you can do to help build the skills they will need to become lifelong readers, and to be successful in whatever paths they choose. Even a newborn can reach out and touch a book, glimpsing the wonder of the world at a very young age.

So make books available to your child as early as you can. Reading aloud is a great way to bond, building your relationship with your child as you explore new worlds together. Books give you a chance to communicate in ways that are new and stimulating. They introduce new ideas, new people, and new experiences in a framework that is not only entertaining but also satisfying, fulfilling, and — even though your child doesn't know it — educational.

Remember your first Golden Book® experience? You can give your child that experience many times over through the wide variety of McKids® books available. Share the reading experience together, and make a difference that will last a lifetime.